ruby moonlight

ruby moonlight

Ali Cobby Eckermann

a novel of the impact of colonisation in mid-
north South Australia around 1880

First published by Magabala Books Aboriginal Corporation, Broome, Western Australia in 2012 Website: www.magabala.com Email: sales@magabala.com

Magabala Books receives financial assistance from the Commonwealth Government through the Australia Council, its arts advisory body. The State of Western Australia has made an investment in this project through the Department of Culture and the Arts in association with Lotterywest.

This manuscript was developed through the support of the State Library of Queenland's 2011 kuril dhagun Indigenous Writing Fellowship, which is part of the State Library's black&write! Indigenous Writing and Editing Project. CAL's Cultural Fund is a proud supporter of the black&write! Indigenous Writing and Editing Project at the State Library of Queensland.

Cover design by Susie Agoston
Cover photograph by Alexandra Agoston
Internal design by Tracey Gibbs
Printed in China at Everbest Printing Company

National Library of Australia Cataloguing-in-Publication entry
Cobby Eckermann, Ali.
Ruby moonlight / Ali Cobby Eckermann.
9781921248511 (pbk.)
A823.4

for my Kami
who disappeared in 1976

and

for all our mob who died
innocent

brave

in true

spirit

Nature

nature
      can
            swirl

like
      a falling
            leaf

sometimes

      turning to
            butterfly

or bereft on the ground

      turning to
            dust

Harmony

in warm afternoon light
a family group rove the plains
murmur delight as
landscapes become familiar

parrots surge their welcome
at the old meeting place
a young woman gathers
wild fruits and berries

her husband the spear maker
admires her supple body
dancing a parody of love
his older brother teases his idolism

his own wife is still lithe
an aged Law holder
the young woman
her only child

in the shade of gum trees
the old woman sings clan songs
as the cooking fires begin
a wombat gifts his soul

sated now the women
dissolve down a cryptic path
under the moons glow
gratitude and joy are danced

Morning

ribbons of campfire smoke
drift to a sunrise sky
as people begin to rise

the spear maker squats by the fire
his weapons hardened over coals
he stands to stretch

his eyes turn to the hillside where
earthen thighs hide a sacred spring
three crows circle near by

he can see the women hurrying
back from the hidden pathway
their movements clumsy in haste

he can see his brother running
from the ochre cliffs signalling
get the spears ready!

fear in their eyes
the women whisper
there is danger here

in gesture language
the old man signals *sshhh!*
the air is wrong!

Warning

the old man and his wife
hold parliament with magpies

within the meeting circle
chatter is warbled with worry

the remainder of the tribe
wait in the shadows

their trust in tribal ways
is absolute

they watch in silence
ready to flee

the meeting erupts
in a bird storm

strange animals and pale men
burst from the river

Ambush

hack
hack
hack
hands
heads
hearts
the clan slaughtered
                    dying
                    dying
                    dead

Silence

the ambience of the morning is ruined
the stench of death fills the air
                love will exist here no more

a young woman sits like rock
 staring at her husband and mother
                their bodies turned tombstone

arid eyes silt with sand
tears will no longer flow
                life is doomed to drought

scrape the images from your eyes
scrape emotion from your heart
            never tell a soul

on the setting sun
she turns to the shadows
            oh kumuna oh kumunari

kumuna – bereavement names for deceased male family members
kumunari – bereavement names for deceased female family members

Shadow

this survivor is a lubra
of the Shadow tribe

who have lived here
since time began

in their passing
will anyone notice?

Birds

senses shattered by loss
she staggers to follow bird song

trust nature

chirping red-browed finches lead to water
ringneck parrots place berries in her path

trust nature

honeyeaters flit the route to sweet grevillea
owls nest in her eyes

trust nature

crimson wattlebirds turn shades of green
blue wrens turn camouflage-brown

trust nature

pied butcher birds lay trinkets in her path
grey fantails flutter a soft revival

trust nature

apostle birds flicker on the edge of her eyes
emus on the horizon stand like arrows

trust nature

the woman turns
follows the emus

Ochre

green and bright blue flits of colour
swirl in a mallee-grey underground
amid constant bird song harmony

along the riverbank bee eaters
dart rainbows around her head
as she paints her body with yellow ochre

splash crimson on bleeding eyes
through the tunnel of darkness
honour the dead

Wander

the desert of her mind has determined wanderings
longer than forty days and nights
lead only by instinct

awakening from the deep trauma of tragedy
she whispers away the nightmares
drives out forbidden memory with smoke

her campfire will remain eternal
conflict between love and hate
will turn to ash

dying embers are carried by coolamon
tradition meanders a well-worn path
along a comforting river

red robins puff their breasts
fanning embers back to flame
a campsite is revealed

at last the woman rests her weariness
rests her grief
and smells rain

Dream

in her sleep she dreams
of a guardian spirit

who sits nearby watching
the young woman's sleeping form

her beauty is unbounded
even in trauma

tight ringlets frame her face
in slumber she looks childlike

her telltale tribal nose is wide
her stature confirms her ancestry

her bosom and buttocks are firm
her stomach is taut

this spirit familiar
is a Shadow too

Shelter

there is a bend along the river
where fish slow in shallow water
   she hears them splash

in the shelter of sandstone
under the overhang hidden by trees
   she slumps in shadowed sorrow

in this overhang a cool breeze blows
language sings on her skin
   she lays within prayer and prospect

there is little movement
days passes without incident
   she tunes to river flow

Wash

her new life starts
this young woman of sixteen years

she washes herself in the stream
scrubs her skin with handfuls of coarse sand

with a stone knife she razors her matted hair
it burns acrid on the embers

the knife slices into her thighs
one sorry mark for each family member

she rubs ash into the wounds
dictated by cultural ritual

blood mingles in the shallow pool
dissolving the pain and the past

she departs among the trees
her long shadow stumbles

Sedge

the woman weaves baskets from sedge
gathered along the banks

bird eggs and lizards
fill her creels

she sits on sheltered sand
by the secluded river cave

a thick grove of wattle bush screens
where water always flows

no-one comes
she is alone

ants on her legs don't bother her
a centipede tramples her toes

she lets the mosquito suck
sandlice dot her skin

a safe feeling
instinct intact

Gifts

the gift of gentle rain
washes over the stony outcrop
she shelters dry on earthen floor

scats of kangaroo
emanate familiar fragrance
the waterfall of rain is scented too

a goanna scurries in to secure shelter
gently panting against the rock face wall
stillness in the woman is complete

one hand grasps the goanna's throat
before it can flinch the neck is snapped
her next meal provided

Intrude

another rain storm
forces her under
the shallow cave

comfort is provided
in the soft staccato
symphony of raindrops

she dozes fading thoughts
forbidden dreams of family
as if a warning

she wakes
with senses shrill
only her eyes move

her nostrils flare
an unusual smell
intrudes

Smoke

from within the wattle bush hide
she observes a smoking ash ghost

it is tall like emu
its face galah pink

seemingly oblivious to the rain
it emits the strange odour

how can it smoke fire
breathe smoke from its mouth

maybe it is a fire man
maybe the rain is putting it out

like water
on hot coals

Bunyip

the lubra follows
through slowing rain

it walks
like magpie

it rubs its chest
like kangaroo

she giggles at its behaviour
hand over her mouth

from behind trees she peers
at mystery man or monster

suddenly it vanishes
into the river bank

Shack

inside the earthen shack
his skin of wet attire
is peeled from pallid skin

teeth clenched he groans
rubs a liniment on bruises
gained from a horse fall

now footsore and flagged he falls
asleep on a rabbit skin rug
in his man-made cave

logs shape three sides
the other rammed earth
it smells reassuring

there are few possessions
a hymnal a faded photograph
a small hand-held mirror

a flute lays discarded
on a bamboo shelf
the silence necessary

Jack

his name is Miner Jack
a solitary life he has chosen

not successful at his trade
he traps pelts to trade for cash

a lean Irish man of thirty
his chin is stubbled red

he is a timid male
in this pioneer country

luck has evaded every choice
in his prospect for comfort and companionship

he lives in the memory of his childhood
before the famine and fighting

oh laddie alas the misfortune
found in a foreign land
yet not the soul song fade
from your mother's tongue of glad

Dark

nightmares from the bed
tossing and turning
untold tales

he snaps from slumber
his green eyes search the dark
his breath slows

he grabs dry clothes
tries to light his pipe
but the flint won't work

he wanders outside
to his campfire
rigid in the sunlight

Hunger

alert eyes watch
him reappear from
the gap in the earthy bank

alert eyes watch
him put fire to the twig
in his mouth until smoke appears

alert eyes watch
him refuel the fire
steam rises like fog

wide eyes watch
him cooking
her stomach rumbles

Beast

after several days his horse returns
Ruby flees in frantic fear

from up a tree she watches
man and beast together

Jack croons like the river
the animal nuzzles his neck

Jack leads the animal
to a grass patch by the river

she watches him rope the legs
still humming his soft lilt

Jack strolls back to his camp
rests on a well-worn tree stump

lights his pipe with precision
smoking with thought

Food

he feels her
before he sees her

she remains hidden watching
he is glad of the company

he begins to offer
plates of food

she accepts the offerings
under cover of night

Friends

good friendships
blossom
slowly

she leaves birds eggs
and dead echidna
by the empty plates

he introduces sugar
she begins to sleep
by his fire

they make love
the first bird sings
a new dawn

Merger

she is glad Jack is
a man of few words

Jack is glad she is
a woman of few needs

in their remoteness
they are heaven

in their remoteness
they are earth

remoteness is essential
in their merger

it is forbidden for Europeans
to fornicate with blacks

Oasis

it is the oasis of isolation
that tolerates this union

neither know
the other's language

they never speak
during the day

only at night
where no-one can hear

he whispers his endearment
ruby moonlight

she is a gem glistening
in night's blackness

Unseen

Ruby loves the smell of earth
in this humble dwelling
a man-made cave

built with logs against the river bank
the moss-covered tin roof
a sanctuary of sorts

a secret room exists
further down the tributary
where she waits as he barters

the price of
pelts with passing buyers
she likes being unseen

it is a safer feeling
than being seen
in full view

Solace

at full moon
he lubs her in his own illiterate way of corse
as a man of few words can

each full moon
he fusses an intimacy for her
small trust is growing

at the river
he washes her hair
eyes shut she sits still

in a fork of a tree
he sets his mirror
to shave his hairy face

Ruby squeals with laughter
watches his face turn from red to pink
she has not seen this behaviour before

laying by the fire to dry
he moves closer to her
enjoys their freshness

in the moonlight
solace is shared
in this forbidden friendship

Beauty

an orange sunrise
spikes up through pink clouds
Ruby smiles at Jack

this is a sign of challenge
maybe a fast goanna
or wild honey in a tall tree

she walks away to bathe
heeding kangaroo tracks
larger than her hands

Ruby walks naked
Jack watches

he is reminded exactly
why he risks her stay

Tempo

          sunrise

days pass

          sunset

          leaves transmute

weeks pass

          shifting stars

          sunshine softens

months pass

          the air cools

        winter returns

Visitor

a soft neigh warns of an arrival
 she slips into shadows
of willows along the river bank

the carriage rounds the last bend
men touch hats in silent greeting
the billy boils

tobacco pouches are passed
cigarettes rolled thin are lit
shadows under hats block out all eyes

we need ya help mate
the words hang on reality without suspense
there's sickness going on cross the river

Jack knows the remainder of the conversation
before it was spoke *ya see any blacks roaming*
best ya kill 'em disease spreading pests

after the departure dust settles
she brings him river water
he sips then spits distaste from his tongue

Signs

Ruby sees signs that mob is near
spot fires form in her eyes

a kookaburra's half call signals
their need for her at dawn

packing essentials in an old flour bag
she steps in to the early morning chill

wood smoke leads her
eager to hear language story

outside their camp Ruby hesitates
watching for her invitation

the movements of these people
are slowed by fatigue

the eyes of these people
are weary from worry

possum is shared
with whispers and warnings

mob pause here
on their winter trek

Whispers

camp smoke whispers
tell story of the *waya*

camp smoke whispers
tell story of the killings

it is harder to hide
old trees are vanishing

it is harder to journey
ancient tracks are risky

Ruby pretends naivety
to these new perils

an old dancer reads Ruby's loss
in her downcast eyes

waya – wire (fence)

Moon

in the moonlight
she sits with this mob

Ruby is Moonlight moiety
of the Shadow tribe

this mob are Cloud people
of the Eastern Shadows

their language and laws are the same
kinship connections form family

the old dancer demands
you my new wife?
leave that colourless man!

Ruby realises this old man watched
her daily ritual with Jack

long before she knew
mob were nearby

Vision

the old dancer visions
his courtship

he is powerful
a master of dance

he is handsome
his torso sculptured

few grey hairs adorn his skull
he carries the strength of the wise

this young woman reminds him
of his missing niece

who never returned
from a hunting trip

he sees her disappearance
in Ruby's eyes

Murmur

amongst the murmurs of the mob
Ruby disregards the dancing

she decides to showcase
Jack to the mob

she wants to justify her safety
with Jack and his simple life

at the cabin she signals
urging him to follow

trepidation meets
Ruby and Jack at the fire

Clouds

Jack watches over the campfire
sees her joy in belonging
hears her laughter in language

her eyes like stars
her teeth like moon
her lips passion

the old man performs
a love dance for Ruby
there is no doubt to his intent

the old dancer's eyes
make Jack scurry back
to the river house

in the silence he feels
 the old man's eyes
scouting from clouds

Jack sits with reality
Ruby will always be a gem
he will always be a miner!

Shame

in her teenage way
Ruby teases the old man
I don't want you!

she feels secure
among the women and children
enjoys their daily gatherings

the old dancer is annoyed
unused to rebuffs of this kind
he shakes his boomerang at her

after in the still of night
he crouches outside the river house
listening to their murmurings

Ritual

it is time to leave
this pausing place

the dancer chants a song
as he climbs the sacred tree

this tree is emu
his grandfather taught him that

it holds the importance of silence
and the power of protection

on a bed of emu feathers
the old man places

possum bones ochre stones
gold nuggets and crystals

courage gifts from other lands
gifts to safeguard the emu spirit

cloak love in this land
guard the woman who is lost
till my autumn return

his obligation fulfilled now
his lust is not

Promise

before he reaches the mob waiting
the old man detours his track

a taller tree stands as sentinel
he climbs against its bleeding bark

placing gems and the magic glass
he stole from the white man

having watched him
peering in and scraping his face

the dancer perches facing the sun
chants a forbidden song

fading butterflies cannot appear
emus will lead to danger eyes
thick with muddy stink

as he climbs down
he speaks his promise

you not for her
I am the one

Depart

sing the songs
dance the dances

share the feast
share the fellowship

songs are sung
dances danced

leave for the coast
leave for saltbush land

mob depart
for new country

Spring

it is lizard season
the weather will turn
green to yellow

a time of plenty
wild berries
wattleseed
river roots

kangaroos will return
when coloured birds
migrate to nest

Ruby roams
along the riverbanks
filling her basket

Jack is often away
for days at a time
setting traps for pelts

a stillness settles
like slow-lifting fog
dulling a morning sun

Caution

roo and fox furs are scarce this season
Jack will be gone for several weeks

Jack secures the cabin entrance
removes all evidence of their tryst

the fear mongers still hunt
roaming blacks to slaughter

Ruby will return to the bush
understands this vacancy as a protective gesture

any proof of their liaison is dangerous
for her safety while he is away

any proof of their liaison is dangerous
for his safety on his return

abo lovers are despised in these parts
fear can fuel the hardest hatred

Kuman

she begins to see him when fishing
or sitting across from her fire
when she is alone

they never speak
although he gestures
when she is nearby

he is extremely tall
similar to her grandfather
with dreadlocked hair

warrior scars on his arms
decorated torso markings
a whimsical twinkle in his eyes

she nicknames him *Kuman*
with respect she will use
no other name

she often forgets
he is not real

this spirit guardian
with strong presence

kuman – an abbreviation of bereavement name

Falling

under open skies a falling star
turns Jack's eyes toward his home

impulsively he packs his gear
starts the return journey

unaware of danger
he walks a unknown path

he staggers like a puppet
although his pile of pelts is small

Jack feels the familiar cold
of failure sting his skin

Mud

Jack considers his future
thoughts of failure babble loud

he notices many emus fleeing his path
the rest of the bush seems at a standstill

with his meagre load
he stumbles into an unseen swamp

brackish water shoots up his nose
he flounders in fetid mud

he feels nauseous at this place
the bush is silent

Green

Jack vomits
the swampy green taste away

he scoops tinder and boils the billy
to rinse his toxic mouth

idle thoughts return to Erin
and his mother's tongue

on the cold winds of night
as the honour of Erin is mourned
an ocean flows from my bosoms
for the promise of golden shores

his eyes life in open prayer
the sun sparkles strange

Fortune

curiosity can kill animals
reptiles mammals and man

the sun sparkles fuels inquisitiveness
guessing the location he climbs

in the treetop breathless
he stares at semi-precious stones

a chunk of gold
and his mirror?

Jack smiles a horizon
my troubles are over

Detour

with springy steps he races past
the track to his camping place
to sell the skins at the store

a small village sits
further down the river
wattle and daub shacks line dirt streets

careless piles of horse manure
 yapping dogs run free
eyes peer from curtains

the shop door rings as he enters
he greets a large breasted woman
her manner loud without voice

in the gloomy shop
the barter is made
for a fistful of cash

Loose

rare money for a rare visit
Jack ambles to the beer house

froth shampoos his new-grown beard
the beer tastes like liquid gold

gold can loosen many a tongue
while silent eyes pry

when the cash is drank
he quietly conjures up a gem

shouting drinks for the bar of men
he coaches ditties to sing

a music-less man stands aloof in the bar
scowling his hatred for the Micks

he decides to surveil
this singing fool

Memory

the man with no music
allergic to lilting laughter
exits the rackety room

the glimpse of that crystal traded
over the beer swilled bar
jolts his memory of gems collected

hunting *diseased stinking blacks*
for civil duty and personal pleasure
a particular ambush sticks in his mind

fizzing with frenzy he fired his gun
with precise accuracy
maiming a black man and his whore

in a fur pouch he found crystals
and their newborn son
that day he lost his music heart

those crystals funded drunken days
an endless torment
of debauchery and violence

he carries his wickedness
in his saddle bag
the mummified hands of the boy

Blur

offered a place to sleep
Jack swags in the stable

on wakening he gulps water
to flush his blurry head

on departing he returns
to the dimness of the store

trades another precious stone
for a small dress

caution is lost as he imagines
his ebony princess

but danger is assured
by the storekeeper's gossipy chin

Shy

focused on her eyes
he hands Ruby the dress

undoes the buttons and clasps
to teach her these things

from the curtain she emerges
her smile shy in new linen

twirling around before him
she giggles with glee

later as she sleeps on his bed
he fondles a hand-made fur pouch

caresses the golden nuggets
nervous of this wealth

before stashing above
the lintel unseen

Broken

entering low spinifex country
much further down the coast
the old dancer falters

his magic powers hear all
warnings from the emu tree
his protection song has been broken

mob sit eyes wide with fear
the meeting (called) is intense
a decision is made

only the old dancer and two warriors
will retrace their travels
to the sacred tree

much danger lays on this tribal track
there is stealth in small numbers
slyness is vital to revenge their law

Torn

Ruby begins to suspect
someone is watching

signs are scattered
bent blades of grass
dislodged bird's nests

fears' chill returns
she finds smoke butts rolled
by a different hand than Jacks

skills honed she risks detection
continues the night time trysts
her ears never resting

Ruby is torn
between companionship
and seclusion

Hate

the man
with no
music in
his heart

suspects
the miner
and lubra
are lovers

silence
rules all
greedy
actions

his need
for gems
inflames
his hate

his plans
simmer
for new
wealth

and two
murders

Scheme

the man with no music has seen enough
he wanders back to his tethered horse

an overgrown laneway leads to a shack
past the cemetery on Ghost Gully Road

two brothers reek in their residence here
a filthy dwelling filled with vermin

easily hired on the promise to kill blacks
they argue nonstop over rights to the *gin*

with rotten teeth smirks
they saddle their unkempt horses

an array of weapons intact
knives and razors and sharp sharp swords

three outcasts are riding today
no conscious plan of action

only murder on their minds
a lone magpie follows

Muddle

Jack is unaware of this hunting
his mind is full of romance

his days are filled in reverie
as new thoughts beckon

during the day he is alone
Ruby always slips away before first light

he cannot decipher her wariness
his muddled mind is too distracted

still the stink of mud pervades his skin
soap and lye cannot remove the stench

when she does not return he sobs a little
fondling and polishing the stones on fur

sleep comes in short bursts
the sickening insomnia has begun

he will wait for her return
echoing his mothers lament

the headland winds will soften my cry
over the rocks of treachery
as the ship sails to lullaby

Cave

she slinks like a dingo
no-one can see her
except a well-trained eye

she hears the soft neigh again
somewhere in the trees behind
coarse voices carry on the breeze

Ruby walks a little quicker
her bare feet make no noise
reaching the river she sees Kuman

from a shady tree he beckons her
leads the way to a cave
Ruby did not know existed

night falls under a new moon
the starlight is enough
to neon cave paintings

Instinct

in the morning Ruby waits
watching the landscape

listening to the wind
and birds

there is no sign of infringement
her heart tells her otherwise

she waits till the sun falls
her heart tells her to stay

when the stars begin to turn
a camp light moves across the plain

the strangers are still
hunting her

Message

she stays in the cave
although Kuman has gone

the first hint of dawn
stirs her dark skin

she sits against the rock face
behind the willow tree screen

her mind sings for Kuman
or any ancestral message

a dingo appears out
of the corner of her eye

looking deeply at her
it turns and vanishes

Ruby decides to follow
with leafy branches from the bush

sweeps her footprints
gone

Cursed

the music-less man and his band
are exhausted from the all night hunt

careless now they camp along the river
mumbling persistence of capture

in their drowsiness they do not see
a flutter of butterflies nearby

a nightmare is cursed in their brains
as Kuman poisons the billy

strange sleep brings rapid breath
eyes jerk rapidly and limb muscles stiffen

upon wakening they ride urgent to reach the hotel
to steady their shingling nerves

hands shaking, whisky spills down their chins
their thirst is unstoppable

in the evening their bloated carcasses
are found by children playing in the river

Jury

townsfolk drag the bodies from the river
the children run to fetch the priest
women watch behind their hands

that night a meeting is held at the hall
kerosene lamps flicker eerie shadows
on community faces filled with fear

the priest refuses burial at the cemetery
unmarked graves will suffice these sinners
their character known to all

the publican fuels fear
retells stories of witchcraft
as slurred by breath now dead

all gather in prayer
the priest presides over
the next hunting party

Misread

Kuman flits across the horizon
he runs through the edge of Ruby's eye

after a short pause
she follows

only when the warriors appear
does Kuman fade to filtering light

but Ruby has located the track
back to the river cabin

confusing the sign
she hastens to Jack

Spear

there is no mistaking
the sound of a spear
hitting its target

the thud shakes
the riverbank cabin
shuddering man and woman

shame in her eyes
she knows
their tryst is over

this time forbidden
by a law stronger
than the white man's

Feathers

a feathery mandala
has been set
around the campfire

after checking the clearing
Jack scoops up the feathers
hurling them into the fire

he returns inside to her
ignoring the warning

he does not want to lose
this ebony joy

he does not want to return
to the existence of loneliness

he does not want to hear
his mother's song fade

but Ruby is already gone
her heart has closed

Empty

Ruby walks naked
to join the old dancer

Jack stays trapped
motionless inside himself

the dress worn once
empty on the floor

Sunset

the old dancer
two young warriors

one lubra looking back
hurry against the skyline

the silhouettes of four
will not be seen

in this land again
for ninety years

in this country
there is sadness

in this sunset
a ruby moonlight

THE END

about the author

Ali Cobby Eckermann is a celebrated Yankunytjatjara/ Kokatha poet and writer. Ali's first collection of poems *little bit long time* was published by the Australian Poetry Centre, in their New Poets series in 2009. The book sold out in months and is printed on demand by Picaro Press.

Her second collection *Kami* was published by Vagabond Press, in their Rare Objects series in 2010. Her first verse novel *His Fathers Eyes* was published by Oxford University Press in 2011, as part of the Yarning Strong educational resource kit.

Ali's poems and short stories have been published in various anthologies, journals and magazines. She has been featured on the Poetry International website. Some of her poems have been translated and published in Croatia, Indonesia, Greece and New Zealand.

She won the 2006 ATSI Survival Poetry Competition and the 2008 Dymocks Red Earth Northern Territory Poetry Award and was Highly Commended for the Marion Eldridge Award in 2009. *Ruby Moonlight* won an inaugural black&write! kuril dhagun Indigenous Writing Fellowship through the State Library of Queensland in 2011.

acknowledgements

I wish to acknowledge the support of my friends
Lionel, Dawn, Kaye, Samia, Sandra and Suzie
for their initial proof reading and feedback; the
black&write! team at kuril dargun SLQ, especially
Ellen; the Broughton River at Koolunga SA and
the many birds who dwell there, that gave me a
glimpse of this story line.

black&write! Indigenous Writing and Editing Project

Established in 2010, and launched by author Boori Monty Pryor and actor Ernie Dingo at the 2010 Cairns Indigenous Arts Fair, black&write! is the first project of its kind. A national project, it is designed to foster Indigenous writing and writers in Australia through the recruitment, training and mentoring of Aboriginal and Torres Strait Islander editors in the development of Indigenous authored manuscripts.

black&write! is made up of the kuril dhagun Indigenous Writing Fellowships and the kuril dhagun Indigenous Editing Mentorships. The Fellowships and Mentorships are named after the kuril dhagun Indigenous Knowledge Centre, located at the State Library of Queensland, South Bank. kuril dhagun is part of the 21-strong network of Indigenous Knowledge Centres located in Cherbourg, Woorabinda and Palm Island and throughout Cape York and the Torres Strait.